SNOW W
and the Seven Dwarfs

Modern Publishing
A Division of Unisystems, Inc. / New York, New York 10022

Once in a far away land, a king and queen had a lovely baby daughter. She was born on a snowy day, and the queen said, "Our daughter is as beautiful and wonderful as each falling snowflake. We shall name her Snow White."

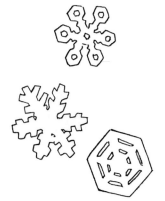

Sadly, the queen died while Snow White was quite young. Some years later, the king decided to marry again. He introduced Snow White to his new wife. "I will be your stepmother, Snow White," the woman said. "I'm sure you and I will get along quite well." She laughed wickedly. Snow White shivered.

The new queen was a powerful magician. She was evil and vain as well. Everyday she would ask her magical mirror, "Looking glass upon the wall, who is fairest of us all?"

"You are the fairest," the mirror would answer, and the queen would smile.

But when the queen came to live with the king and Snow White, the mirror's answer changed.

"Who is the fairest in all the kingdom?" the queen asked her mirror.

"Snow White is the fairest!" the mirror answered.

As Snow White's lovely face appeared in the magical mirror, the queen flew into a rage.

"She will not be the fairest in the kingdom for long!" vowed the queen, and she called for a huntsman. "Take my stepdaughter far into the woods until she is outside of the kingdom. Then leave her there," she told the huntsman. The huntsman tried to protest, but the queen insisted, "Do as I say or I'll have your head and your wife's, too. You are not to tell anyone about this!"

The huntsman did as the queen ordered and left Snow White in the woods, unable to find her way home.

After much wandering, Snow White came upon a small cottage. She knocked on the door, but no one answered. Snow White was cold and tired, so she let herself in.

Once inside, Snow White fell sound asleep. She didn't hear the owners of the cottage come home.

Seven dwarfs lived in the cottage. They were surprised to find Snow White when they came home from their long day's work.

Snow White woke when she heard the stamping of their heavy boots. After a moment's fright she saw their gentle smiles and knew she was among friends. Snow White told the dwarfs all about her evil stepmother.

"Please, stay here with us!" the dwarfs cheered.

"Thank you! I will take good care of all of you," Snow White promised.

Snow White loved taking care of the dwarfs and their home.

She didn't know, however, that the huntsman had not taken her far enough into the woods and that she was still within her father's kingdom. But the queen knew. The mirror still said Snow White was the fairest in the kingdom and the queen was furious. She decided to get rid of Snow White once and for all.

With her magical powers, the queen put an evil spell on a silk ribbon. Then she disguised herself as an old peddler and went to the dwarfs' cottage, where she tricked Snow White into buying the ribbon.

No sooner had Snow White tried on the ribbon
than she fell to the floor in a deep sleep.

Luckily, the dwarfs took the ribbon off as soon as they found her, and Snow White woke up.

"You must be more careful of strangers," the dwarfs scolded.

But when the queen again came in disguise,
Snow White forgot the dwarfs' warning and
accepted an apple.

The apple was poisoned and after one small bite,
Snow White fell to the ground.

This time the dwarfs did not know how to save
their beloved friend. It appeared Snow White would
never wake again.

Sadly, the dwarfs placed Snow White in a beautiful glass box filled with snow-white roses. They carried her to a peaceful spot in the forest. Just as they were saying goodbye, a prince on a fine white horse stopped to see what was happening.

The prince gazed at Snow White and he was so overcome by her beauty that he bent and kissed her gently. He wished she could be his bride.

As he did so, Snow White's eyes began to flutter and she woke from her deep sleep.

The dwarfs danced and sang happily while Snow White told the prince what happened. He asked for her hand in marriage, and Snow White accepted.

The dwarfs followed Snow White and her prince to the edge of the forest. Snow White promised to come back and visit them often.

Then Snow White and the prince, rode off to live happily ever after.